P9-CFF-571

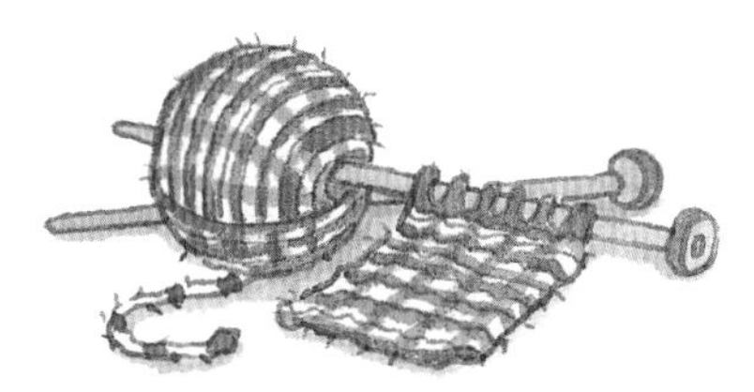

For Molly Melling
Thanks Mom

JUST LIKE MY MOM
by David Melling

First published in the UK
© 2004 by Hodder Children's Books

This 2008 edition published by Sandy Creek,
by arrangement with Hodder Children's Books.

All rights reserved. No part of this publication may be reproduced,
stored in a retrieval system, or transmitted, in any form or by any means,
electronic, mechanical, photocopying, recording, or otherwise,
without prior written permission from the publisher.

Copyright © David Melling 2004

Sandy Creek
122 Fifth Avenue
New York, NY 10011

ISBN-13: 978 1 4351 1417 3

A catalogue record of this book is available from the British Library.

Printed and bound in China

1 3 5 7 9 10 8 6 4 2

The right of David Melling to be identified as the author
and illustrator of this Work has been asserted by him
in accordance with the Copyright, Designs and Patents Act 1988.

Just Like My Mom

David Melling

This is my mom.

In the morning I always wake early...

…just like my mom.

I y-a-w-n,

and g*rrr*oan,

and I'm ready
for the day...

…just like my mom.

If I hurt myself,

or argue with someone,

or get upset...

…my mom makes me feel better.

And when
I'm a silly
little monkey...

I say ‘sorry’…

…just like my mom.

When I'm bored my mom
doesn't like it.

She says,

'Why don't you *do* something?'

But when I do something...

she says,

'Just sit still for five minutes!'

My mom helps
me make things.
She knows
everything.

And her ideas are *so* interesting…

...*everyone* **wants to play!**

Sometimes I have good ideas of my own…

But Mom says,

'Dry games are better!'

That's typical…

…just like
my mom.

There's an old squiggly
tree which is my
favorite place
for climbing with
my friends.

At the end of the day,
we all want to be somewhere
quiet, safe and warm,
with someone...

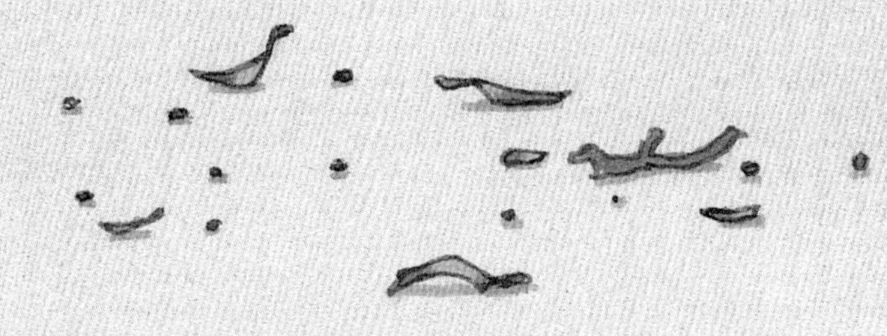

...just like my mom.